Bantam Books in the Choose Your Own Adventure® series
Ask your bookseller for the books you have missed

Also by R.A. Montgomery
TRIO: REBELS IN THE NEW WORLD

SMOKE JUMPER

BY R.A. MONTGOMERY

ILLUSTRATED BY LESLIE MORRILL

BANTAM BOOKS

NEW YORK · TORONTO · LONDON · SYDNEY · AUCKLAND

RL 4, age 10 and up

SMOKE JUMPER
A Bantam Book / March 1991

*CHOOSE YOUR OWN ADVENTURE® is a registered trademark of
Bantam Books, a division of Bantam Doubleday Dell Publishing Group,
Inc. Registered in U.S. Patent and Trademark Office and elsewhere.*

Original conception of Edward Packard

*Cover art by Kevin Johnson
Interior illustrations by Leslie Morrill*

ISBN 0-553-28861-X

Published simultaneously in the United States and Canada

*Bantam Books are published by Bantam Books, a division of Bantam Double-
day Dell Publishing Group, Inc. Its trademark, consisting of the words
"Bantam Books" and the portrayal of a rooster, is Registered in U.S. Patent
and Trademark Office and in other countries. Marca Registrada. Bantam
Books, 666 Fifth Avenue, New York, New York 10103.*

PRINTED IN THE UNITED STATES OF AMERICA

OPM   0 9 8 7 6 5 4 3 2 1

SMOKE JUMPER

__WARNING!!!__

Do not read this book straight through from beginning to end. These pages contain many different adventures that you may have as a smoke jumper, fighting fires in the Pacific northwest. From time to time as you read along, you will be asked to make a choice. Your choice may lead to success or disaster!

The adventures you have are the results of your choices. You are responsible because you choose! After you make a choice, follow the instructions to see what happens to you next.

Think carefully before you make a decision. Becoming one of an elite group of fire fighters can be fun, but it can also be dangerous. Even if you do make it through the training program and parachute into a forest fire, you may not be able to extinguish the flames in time.

Good luck!

You've been lying awake for almost an hour when the early morning sun falls upon your tent, flooding it with a golden light. Reaching up, you pull the tent flaps aside, letting in the cool morning air. You take a deep breath, the smell of pine filling your lungs. Then you tug the zipper on your sleeping bag, running it halfway down the bag.

With as much energy and enthusiasm as you can muster at this hour of the morning, you welcome the new day that lies ahead. "Rise and shine," you say. "Rise and—"

A voice from the tent next to yours interrupts you. "You sound like one of those TV evangelists! Thank you, thank you, thank you."

"You know, you really know how to start the day right, Bill. Thank you. Thank you very much," you reply.

The tent is dome shaped, and there is just enough room for you to stand up inside it, but not quite. You climb out of your down-filled sleeping bag and manage to pull on your clothes—shorts, T-shirt and a light shirt. Then you step out into the brilliant dawn, the sun cresting the range of mountains to the north. Some of them still have snow hiding in the shadowy flanks, and once again you are taken aback by the beauty of the scene. If only you could relax and enjoy yourself.

Scheduled today is your first actual training jump—the two of you have enrolled in a special jump unit assigned to combat forest fires in the mountains of the Pacific northwest.

Turn to page 2.

"Do you think we'll really jump today?" Bill asks.

"I don't know," you say. "Weather looks good. We're ready and so are Patty, Joe, and Michael. I'd say it's a go."

Just hearing your own words once again gives you a shiver of excitement tinged with real fear. Up until now everything has been theory and training; but now it's time to take the next step. On your next flight, you will jump out of the plane and really parachute.

The weeks of tough physical work and practice, as well as practical things like the proper packing of your chute, have centered your thinking on the life of a smoke jumper. You are ready and eager, but you are also scared. Worse almost than the real fear of the first jump is the fear that you might freeze, that your friends will see you as a coward. After one month of training, now comes the real test. Fighting fires comes later, maybe, assuming you pass. You try your best not to be too doubtful and focus on the importance of your newly acquired skills.

"We'd better jump. I'm getting tired of this waiting," Bill says, bringing you back to reality.

The conversation ends, and you busy yourself with the details of cleaning up the tent and the campsite. The others are just emerging from their tents, and their chatter is very similar to Bill's and yours.

Go on to the next page.

Breakfast, as usual, is mammoth: pancakes, eggs, bacon, toast, cereal, juice, and tea. The cook, a skinny guy named Tomas, loves to see everybody eat. You are only too happy to comply.

"Dig in!" Tomas says. "What's with all of you, anyway? You eat like birds. You're gonna be eating smoke soon, so you'd better have some real food now while you can."

You're tempted to tell him that birds actually eat more food each day than humans do in proportion to their body weight, but you resist the temptation. He's really very nice, and he's always encouraging everyone, downplaying the dangers and the difficulties.

The other tables are empty once again; the veteran jumpers are out on a fire on a fork of Bear Creek, some eighty miles from camp. They've been gone for three days, and the reports are that they're having trouble. Several times during the last few days you've thought that you smelled smoke in the air. When you asked Tomas, he nodded and said that you were probably right.

"See them clouds, those dark smudgy ones?" he asked. "Well, more than likely that's smoke from the fire, coming from the river down in one of those steep valleys. Some say it was lit."

"What do you mean?" you ask, knowing his answer.

"Just that. Someone set the fire. Happens, and when it does, it's nasty."

"But why? Why would someone do something like that?"

Go on to the next page.

4

"Why's not important. You just have to deal with them, get them out. When they're burning, they're burning," Tomas says. "Most fires are caused by nature. You know, lightning strikes and does its work. And when it's dry like this summer, we're in for some hot times."

As you finish your breakfast, Henry Brouillard arrives in his 4x4 pickup, a cloud of road dust kicking up behind him. Henry is in charge of the summer program. Although he is tough, he is fair and truly interested in his job and the welfare of all his jumpers. At forty-six, he is trim and athletic. He stands over six feet, has a beard, salt-and-pepper hair, and is rugged looking and powerful.

Turn to page 14.

Porky and Brouillard were the last ones out of the plane, but they were in free-fall long enough to catch up with the rest of you. You see them hanging from their chutes, and they signal to you, giving you the thumbs-up sign.

Two assistant jumpmasters are on the ground with battery-powered bullhorns. They are giving directions and encouragement. "Watch the wind. Hey, you, more to the right! Good job, all of you. You're doing just fine."

You watch as the first two jumpers touch ground. The first one does it textbook style, stepping down, his chute emptied of air. The second is not as fortunate. He hits the ground hard and tumbles, being dragged a few yards before his chute spills its air.

Turn to page 109.

6

You reason that there is security in numbers, so you decide to get the others involved. The tents are spread out in the area surrounding the cabins. Some are in the woods, others near the small lake. In the dark with the moon covered by heavy clouds, you find it hard to locate all of them easily.

"Hey, wake up. We need help. Keep your voice down," you whisper at each tent. Some wake easily, others are really hard to rouse. Soon you have them all in a group in the woods.

"This is the deal. Some people, don't ask me who they are, are sabotaging our gear and equipment. Porky is keeping an eye on them over by the parachute shed. They have Bill hostage."

All at once there is a flurry of conversation, some concerned, some playfully skeptical. The only emergency for most of them is that they're losing sleep and wish to get back to their tents.

The babble is irritating, but you try to be patient. Time is slipping by, and Bill's life is in danger. Why can't these people get it together? you ask yourself.

"Okay, listen up! Those that want to help over here." You motion to your side. "Those that don't go back to your tents. But I'm telling you, this is no joke."

Suddenly the seriousness in your voice catches hold, and everyone shuts up.

Turn to page 60.

8

"Okay! Piece of cake. All of you will do fine, no problem!" says Brouillard, but his attempt to calm you down doesn't really work. Your stomach feels like it's no longer a part of your body; you can almost hear your heart beating.

Suddenly you flash back to the time when your dad took you to an amusement park and you went on a roller coaster called the Ride of Death. For the whole week before you left, all your little sister could do was talk about that ride. By the time you got there you were so terrified all you could think of was getting back home safe and sound. The Ride of Death was pretty traumatic, and from that day on you've always hated amusement parks. You are reminded of that day, and something inside you, a premonition perhaps, tells you not to jump. It's only natural to have second thoughts, you realize, but right now it doesn't look like you can go through with it.

*If you decide to abort the jump,
turn to page 98.*

*If you decide to go ahead with the jump,
turn to page 64.*

"This is all going to be very easy," the man announces. "We're going to wait until dawn. Your friends are going to get up as usual. Porky, here, will tell them it's jump time. You will join them. Once inside the plane—"

He doesn't have a chance to finish his sentence—Tomas bursts through the door and flings himself onto the man. They crash to the floor, but the fight is all over before it begins. Moments later the man is trussed up.

"Tomas, what happened?" you ask, stunned by the suddenness of the event.

"These guys are some kind of terrorists for hire," he says. "They specialize in environmental damage—hold forests hostage, water supplies. They're sick, really sick. They use their terrorism to extort money from communities or governments. At least that's their plan, to torch a forest unless they get money."

Turn to page 66.

The engine, as if in agony, groans and coughs. You turn the key again and listen to it growl and sputter. Then it catches, erupting into its full, impressive sound.

"Okay! Let's get rolling!" you shout, psyching yourself up.

The gearshift is on the floor. It takes you a while to locate reverse, but when you do, the big truck jerks into action, moving backward and almost clipping one of the 4x4's.

Moments later you are rolling down the dirt road, out of the camp, and picking up speed. As soon as you are clear of the camp, you switch on the lights.

"Now where do I go?" you say, addressing the space around you. "I don't know where the police are, I don't even know where anything is."

Turn to page 20.

12

"I'll go, Chief," you say, somewhat surprised by your own conviction.

"Me too," Bill shouts, standing up. The others seem relieved that there are enough volunteers. They remain silent, turning their attention back to the instructor and the problems of landing in a burn zone.

"Okay, follow me. And thanks. I appreciate what you've given up. I'll do my best to make it up to you."

Moments later the three of you are bouncing along a dirt road in his 4x4, headed to a heli-pad where the two Alouette helicopters are parked. This is the first time you've ever been inside one of these French jet helicopters, well-known for their ability to perform at high altitudes in the Alps of Europe. Quickly you load your gear into the far one. With Brouillard at the controls, you lift off the pad, and like a dragonfly, swerve into the air and head for the site of the first fire.

You feel like a veteran now that you have had your first successful jump, but you caution yourself against getting too cocky. Jumping is dangerous, just like riding a motorcycle or climbing mountains. You are risking your life. You must take nothing for granted, be prepared, and concentrate, you remind yourself among the noise of the rotors.

Turn to page 91.

"Hey! You okay?" Brouillard asks, coming up to you with a quizzical look. There is something about him that reminds you of your dad; it's not a physical resemblance, it's more his way with people and his instinctive understanding of those your age. He's someone you can trust, you feel.

"Yeah, I'm fine," you say. "Smoke got to me for a moment. I guess I'm still a little excited from the jump."

"Well, come on over. I want to introduce you to these guys," Brouillard says. Bill, you notice, has already walked over and introduced himself to the two rangers.

Before you get a chance to shake hands with the two men, you are interrupted by the sound of the walkie-talkie, hanging from the limb of a pine in the clearing.

"Ranger Three! Ranger Three! Mayday! Need a med-evac upriver. Do you read?"

"Loud and clear. Standing by," Ranger Three replies.

"One man down. Looks like smoke inhalation. We need Brouillard and his copter. Our other one's out."

Brouillard nods assent.

"He's on his way. He'll meet you at base camp over by Rocky Ridge."

"Negative. Further upstream. Tell him to be careful. It's gonna be tight getting in. We need help fast. Vital signs are weak."

Turn to page 79.

14

Jumping down from the truck, Henry strides across the open ground, grinning and yet looking determined at the same time.

"Okay! Gather round everybody. This is what you've all been waiting for. It's also what you've been dreading," he says, chuckling. There is a sprinkle of nervous laughter, but not from you. "Today, at 0900 hours, you will make your first jump! As you know, you need ten jumps to qualify as a smoke jumper."

A whoop of excitement goes up, and there is a lot of back slapping and poking in the ribs from the group of soon-to-be jumpers such as yourself.

"Quiet down. Have your gear ready and meet me at the airfield, ready to go, in ten minutes."

Three hours later you are climbing with the others up an aluminum ladder into the DC–3 transport plane that is used as a jump ship. As you climb aboard, the starboard engine is already ticking over and the prop wash gives everyone a good fanning. It takes a few seconds for your eyes to adjust to the dark interior of the plane. Inside, the ten of you, plus Brouillard and the jumpmaster called Porky, take your seats. Porky checks with the ground crew, then closes the door. Nobody is talking. They all are either staring at the floor or double-checking their gear.

Turn to page 59.

Turn to page 28

"Milt, I'd love to go on with this discussion," you say, "but it's getting late. I'd better be on my way if I'm going to find your friend."

Milt gets up, too. "Got a point there, kid. Time's a-wastin'." He wraps the remaining cheese in the paper and hands it to you after you pick up the orange rinds and put them in your pack. "You take this. It's kind of my way of saying 'thanks' for going after Tim."

"Thanks. Well, take care," you say, moving on. You're not sure why, but for some reason you feel nervous around this man. As soon as you are out of his sight, you stop, look around, and check to see if Milt has followed you. He doesn't seem to have.

"I'm just a little spooked," you say to yourself out loud. "I'm sure he's just a regular guy. A little strange perhaps, but . . . come to think of it, maybe I should radio in a report to Haven. It would be good to let someone know, in case I get into trouble."

You're about to make the call when you stop yourself. Perhaps you're being a little too hasty. Maybe you should just continue with your patrol and look for Milt's friend and not get yourself all worked up over nothing.

If you decide to radio Haven and report your meeting with Milt, turn to page 94.

If you decide not to radio a message, and continue on your way, turn to page 106.

Bill looks over at you questioningly; you shake your head no. After all, the main reason you enrolled in the training course was to learn how to jump. You like Brouillard and don't wish to see him stranded. If no one else volunteers, then you will. Fortunately three people speak up. Brouillard picks two, and moments later they are on their way in his 4x4.

Getting on with the class, Porky stands up on a table in the mess hall. "Okay, you jumpers. Well done! I've seen a lot of first jumps, and you were all great. Every single one of you."

There is a lot of cheering and hooting. Porky lets the roar subside before he continues. "We're going to debrief all of you. We'll do it alphabetically. Everyone outside, back to your instructors!"

Turn to page 36.

The topo is spread out on the rocky ground, and Milt points to a route marked in yellow that leads through the forest, coming from a road over by an abandoned ranch. It is within the same territory as the fires that Brouillard flew to for the med-evac. The pale yellow line snakes along until it almost reaches the spot where you now sit.

"I'd say he is stumbling around in the brush about here," Milt says, pointing to a region that Brouillard said posed potential danger if the fire got out of hand. "Tim's a little spooky. He's a city boy, always prepared for trouble, you know. Oh, by the way, he's armed. Carries a magnum. It's a silly little thing. I don't like guns much myself, but we're all different, right?"

Your instincts tell you that there's more here than meets the eye. Play it cool, you advise yourself, play it real cool. "What do you do back in Los Angeles, Milt?" you ask, trying to sound innocent.

Milt busies himself, cutting the cheese with a hunting knife, then hands you a hunk on the blade.

"Oh, I'm a dabbler, you might say. A little of this, a little of that. Real estate mostly. That's the racket to be in these days."

Turn to page 78.

Following your instincts, you head onto the paved two-lane road and drive until you come upon the first house, almost eleven miles away.

A grumpy man answers the door; but once you explain to him what is going on, he is all help.

He telephones the police, and they order you to stay where you are so no one gets hurt. All you can do now is wait.

Twenty minutes later you hear the unmistakable sound of helicopters. You can't restrain yourself any longer. You thank the man for his kindness and help, and soon you are back in the truck, heading for the camp.

Unfortunately, about five miles from the camp, your truck sputters and rolls to a halt. You don't know what the problem is, and you don't have time to figure it out. One thing's for sure, you're on your feet now.

Turn to page 77.

"You want to leave a note with me in case I run into him?" you query.

"Well, I was hoping you wouldn't mind helping me out by going into the canyon to find him for me." Milt says. "I'm afraid he'll get really worried if I don't show up, and I've got to leave here this afternoon. What do you say? Will you do it?"

The sun is warm and the fatigue of the day settles into your bones. Another decision is the last thing you want to make right now. As you sit, you realize you have to go up into that canyon anyway. Maybe he is one of the people reported to be wandering around up there. But if he isn't, can you really spend your time looking for him while you are on an assignment?

*If you agree to look for Milt's friend,
turn to page 76.*

*If you decide that he is asking too much,
turn to page 45.*

Turn to page 83

"Hello?" you ask, tentatively.

"Keep quiet. It's me, Bill," comes back a whisper.

"What's up? Jump got you excited? Can't sleep either?"

"No, but it's more than that. Something strange is going on here."

"The only thing strange around here is you," you reply. With that you unzip the tent flap and step out into the night. The clouds are covering the moon and stars. It's hard to see, but you can make out Bill's shape. "So, what's up?"

"Well, you might think I'm nuts, but—" Bill stops in mid-sentence, grabs you by the arm, and pushes you behind the tent. Two figures rush by.

"See those two?" he asks. "I was up, prowling around. I was hungry, actually, looking for something to eat in the mess hall. Tomas sometimes leaves leftovers out. That's when I saw them."

"Who?" you ask.

"You never give me a chance to tell a story."

"That's because you drone on so much. Get to your point. Who were they?"

"That's it. I never saw them around here before. But they sure looked like they knew what they wanted, and what they were doing."

Turn to page 89.

"Come on, Bill. Let's not be heroic," you say. "Let's get Porky."

"I'll go after them," Bill says. "You get Porky." Before you can argue, he is gone.

"It's always up to me," you mumble to yourself, heading for Porky's cabin.

Porky, Tomas, Brouillard, and the other instructors all live in separate log cabins built during the depression in the nineteen-thirties. Everyone else lives in tents.

All the lights are out. You feel a bit foolish waking them up; it's probably just some kids messing around, you think: But reason gets the better of you. Everyone here knows just how important the equipment is. No one would mess around with that stuff unless they were up to no good.

You rap lightly on the old wooden door of Porky's cabin. "Porky? Hey, Pork, you in there?" you ask. But there is no answer. You try again, to no avail. Screwing up your courage, you try the doorknob. It's unlocked, and you push gently on it. The door swings softly on its hinges. You enter, peering into the darkness, and see a light coming from under the bedroom door at the back of the cabin.

There's something odd here, you say to yourself. "Hey, Porky!" you call once again, your voice louder this time.

Turn to page 73.

"One move and this jumper's history," a sharp voice says.

You and Porky freeze where you are. Bill stands rigidly, eyes forward. His fear is most evident.

"I don't think they know that there are two of us here," you whisper into Porky's ear. "You could melt into the shadows and get Tomas and the others." Porky thinks for a moment, nods his head, and whispers back, "It's risky, but it's up to you. That leaves you exposed, left to deal with these creeps. There's no telling who they are or what they want."

Obviously you don't want to remain behind. But if they don't know Porky is with you, it might be worth the risk to have him run and get help. On the other hand, perhaps *you* should go for help. Porky is older than you—he should be able to take care of himself and protect Bill. The longer you wait, though, the less of an option you have. Whatever your decision, you must react quickly.

If you tell Porky to go, turn to page 56.

If you decide you should go, turn to page 54.

26

At that moment you hear the sound of rotor blades overhead. Your heart does a quick somersault as Milt ducks for cover and a Colt magnum suddenly appears in his hand. Instinctively you dive for a shallow ravine on the opposite side of the trail from where Milt has taken cover.

"Take that!" Milt screams, firing his weapon toward the sky. He keeps on firing, the sounds ripping loudly through the late afternoon air.

Scurrying like a crab, you make your way along the ravine until you are out of sight. The copter settles down, and Milt is up and running. You remain hidden by brush and rock, not daring to make a move.

Turn to page 55.

You decide to go on patrol and warn the campers who might be up on the rim. Haven briefs you on the area, providing you with a topographic map. He circles an area of about four miles where the group of campers are reported to have been seen. He also gives you a radio, but he cautions you, "The range on this thing is limited. It's an old model and the batteries are weak. You can't really rely on it. Stay out of trouble. Have you got rations?"

"Well, not really. I have enough for today, I guess. A sandwich, a candy bar, a couple of oranges."

"What about a canteen? Have you got a parka or a poncho?" he asks.

You shake your head.

"Here, take this. It's the only one I have." Heaven hands you a windbreaker. It's forest green, a color that blends in too well with your surroundings. If you were in trouble out in the woods or the mountains, you might never be spotted. Your dad always believed in using bright colors in the outdoors. He said it was an extra margin of safety, and you never knew when it would be needed. You do not approve of the color of this sweater, but given the circumstances it will have to do.

Go on to the next page.

"You can use this canteen. Remember, sunset is close to eight o'clock. It's almost one right now. Try to get back before dark, okay? We'll meet you here," Haven instructs.

"No problem," you reply, anxious to get on your way. You can't believe the time. It seems like a week has passed since you got up this morning. Looking around, you realize Bill has already left with the other ranger to help with the fire.

Turn to page 88.

"Well, he's no buddy of mine, and this is the proof," Tim says, rubbing the lump on his skull.

"Tell me what happened exactly," you ask, washing the blood from his face with a bandana moistened from your canteen.

"He hit me on the head with a rock and stole my gun. I was groggy but not quite out. His last words were something like, 'This should teach you never to play with firearms.' Pretty weird, huh?" Tim is now sitting up. He looks better; color is returning to his face.

Suddenly you smell smoke and hear the rush and crackle of fire. Above the noise, you hear a voice, distant but clear, "Too bad, suckers! It's the end of the rainbow for you both!"

You stare in the direction of the voice coming from behind a ridge. The wind fans the flames, and the heat rises and surges, surrounding you.

Desperately you key the radio and call, "MAYDAY! MAYDAY!" but all you get in return is static.

The End

You nod in agreement. Haven's mention of the Old Coyote makes you stop and think for a moment. You remember reading that the Indians believed that the Old Coyote was a powerful spirit, responsible for all sorts of mischief. He is both a trickster and a teacher, and the Indians saw him as a reflection of themselves. They were entertained and educated by stories of the Old Coyote, passing them down from generation to generation.

Just what did Haven mean by mentioning the Old Coyote, you wonder. Maybe he was trying to tell you you must see things with different eyes and prepare for the unexpected, while still remaining true to your purpose, you decide. All that behind you, however, it's time for you to move on once again. There's still a fire for you to get under control.

The End

Above you, the afternoon clouds have moved into their usual position. The promise of rain is only that, a promise. The wind picks up a bit. That could mean trouble for the fire. The wind not only feeds it but carries it along. You'll have to keep the direction of the wind in mind as you patrol.

The route on the topo map is pretty straightforward. You follow a stream for almost a mile, finding the trail easily. The trees are old and well spaced. There isn't too much underbrush. As you walk, you find it is quite pleasant to be on your own, away from the excitement of the jump school and the noise of the others, and you relax as your breathing settles down into its natural rhythm.

A mile or so later the stream hooks left, and you start to head uphill.

Turn to page 58.

"He's not kidding," Porky says. "We're in the plane. Our hands are tied, and we're on the static line without parachutes. There are three of them with us plus the pilot."

"What about Tomas, Marc, and the others?" you query.

"Roger for all of them. They were already in the plane when we got here."

"Who are these people?" you ask.

"That's all the time you get," a hard voice replies. "Who we are is of no concern to you. We have a job to do, and you are going to help us. Your payment is the safe return of your friends. Failure to comply will result in their release one by one over the drop zone."

You hear the big DC-3 overhead making a large circle, its motors pulling it through the cloud cover. Moments dangle with painful intensity.

"The green light is going on. They're preparing us to jump," comes a panicked voice.

"Okay, okay! We'll do it. Wait."

Turn to page 80.

"The police. That's it. I'll just call the police. Why didn't I do that before?" you say to yourself out loud. There are telephones in the office, as well as on the wall of the mess hall. The mess hall is the easiest to get to.

Moments later you are there, lifting the receiver and dialing. "Operator, I need—hey, what's with this thing?" The line is dead. You slam the phone back on the hook. Heart pounding, you race to the office. The door is locked. Without hesitating, you grab a rock, smash the window, and reach in to unlock the door. The phone there is dead, too.

Frantically you search for the radio phones. When you find the rack where they are stored, you're not surprised to find them gone. What to do now? you wonder.

As you stand there, wondering what to do next, several options come to you. You can either run back to the tents and wake the others, return to Porky and see what you can do, or grab a vehicle and drive to the police for help. All these plans sound good, but they're all equally risky, too.

*If you decide to wake the others,
turn to page 6.*

If you return to Porky, turn to page 63.

*If you decide to take a vehicle and get the
police, turn to page 65.*

Outside, the late morning sun is intense, and the smell of pine is heavy and wonderful. You feel that every breath of air that you take is charged with life. You just can't get enough of it. Having completed your jump, you feel more powerful than you have ever felt before. Enrolling in this summer program was the best idea you ever had. Your dad sure would be proud of you. For a few moments you let yourself think about the times you had with him, but you stop yourself before the sadness overcomes you.

Tomas has prepared a special treat for everyone in honor of the first jump. Clanging a piece of angle iron that hangs from the rafters of the mess hall porch, he shouts, "Come and get it!" just like in the movies. A pile of freshly made doughnuts, brownies, and cookies sits on the center table.

Turn to page 46.

Deciding to fight the fire, you surprise Bill by the way you speak right up. He just sort of shrugs his shoulders. You hope you didn't hurt his feelings, but one thing your father always stressed was to speak your mind and stand up for what you thought and what you believe in. "Don't be afraid, and don't do things just because you think that's what other people want. Do what you think is right." You can hear his voice as though he were still alive, and it brings you both comfort and sadness.

Haven radios to the firefighting team. "This is Haven. Send Pete to patrol the ridge for pilgrims. I'm going to the fire with two of the new trainees. Over."

"Sure thing, chief, 10–4."

Turn to page 83.

Not fifteen minutes up the trail, you get into a zone of heavy smoke. Eyes stinging, nostrils clogging, you cough and hack, wondering how you'll be able to keep moving further on. You didn't expect it to be this bad. For a few moments you consider turning back, but then from out of the smoke comes Haven.

"Hey! Where were you guys? I turned around and you were gone. Come, we need help. This fire is nastier than we thought."

"Yeah, but—"

"No time for *buts*, let's move it. Where's Bill?"

"He's back about a quarter mile. We saw—."

Haven cuts you off again. "Well, get him!"

"Haven, will you listen for a minute?" Your voice is firm, and you finally get his attention.

"Okay, what is it?"

"Like I was trying to say, we saw a man back on the opposite ridge. He was waving a shirt or something. We think he needs help."

"Why didn't you tell me?"

"I've been trying to, Haven. I've been trying." You are beginning to lose patience with this man. Officials can be so official, you think. "So, what should we do?"

"Make tracks, what else! Check it out. You and Bill see what you can do." With that he melts back into the smoke as though he were an apparition. You don't like this at all; Haven was less than helpful.

Turn to page 103.

Once on the ridge, you stop for a moment to rest and get your bearings.

"Hey, what's that?" Bill asks, pointing to the far ridge at what appears to be a figure.

"Looks like a person. But what's he doing?" you reply.

"He seems to be signaling. Maybe he needs help."

The figure is waving a shirt and moving back and forth within a ten- or twelve-foot space. You try to shout, but it is too far, and the noise of the stream blocks your voice from traveling. You figure that hiking to the ridge would take you about fifty minutes or so out of your way.

"What do you think, Bill? Should we investigate?"

"Well, it's not that far. But maybe we should turn this one over to Haven."

You look around, but Haven is out of your line of sight. You could try and catch up with him but maybe you can take the situation into your own hands and see what the man wants.

*If you decide to help the man,
turn to page 107.*

If you catch up with Haven, turn to page 101.

42

Looking at your watch, you decide it's time for you to head back. "This is what they call a real wild-goose chase," you say out loud, your anger mounting along with the dreadful self-criticism that goes with it. "I guess Bill was right after all."

It takes you longer to get back than it did going up, but eventually you catch up with Haven, Bill, and the others. Haven takes you aside and you fear the worst, expecting a lecture at the very least.

"Hey, look, I appreciate what you did," Haven says. "You took a risk, and I would have done the same. But you gotta watch out, though. The 'Old Coyote' will get you if you don't. I sure would like to catch that joker. Whoever he is, he's in for trouble when we find him."

Turn to page 31.

But what in the world could their reasons be? What would be in it for them? You do your best to erase these thoughts. They couldn't be involved. Screwing around with those parachutes would be murder. Then suddenly it hits you with a double blow—you could have been murdered! The image of your chute failing to open is too graphic and too awesome for you to dwell on. You shudder at the thought.

Turn to page 35.

"I'm sorry, but I can't look for your friend," you say to Milt. "I have an assignment I must complete. I'll warn your friend if he's in my search zone and I run into him, but I can't promise you that I will find him."

"I understand," Milt says. "Well, as I was saying, I've got things to do, places to go, people to see. You take care. And watch out for wild animals. People get hurt in the woods, ya know." He turns to leave, giving you a half sort of wave.

"Hey, wait a minute. I've got an idea," you say.

"Yeah, what?" he asks, standing where he is, his face still turned away from you.

"I've got a radio. I can call in and have a helicopter come and search the area. Your friend might be in the fire zone. In that case he might be in danger."

"No! No, that's not necessary. He's all right, I'm sure of that. Don't want to get too many people involved," Milt says, somewhat nervously.

"Hey, no problem," you reply, removing the radio and beginning to key it.

"I said no," Milt says, taking the radio from your hand firmly with a grip that surprises you. "Let's just put this little thing away before there's trouble. Be a good kid now, and listen to me, all right?"

Turn to page 51.

The debriefing takes up most of the afternoon, especially when you are as anxious as you are to jump again. Porky is a good teacher and someone to be respected in his own low-key way. The session with him speeds by, and you are surprised at how much you learn just by talking about the jump and what it felt like.

"Tomorrow we'll jump again. Take the afternoon off and get some rest tonight," he tells you.

At night, however, a storm system blows in from the west, and huge, cumulous clouds build up over the mountains. Wind swoops down on the camp, and the first few drops of rain spatter into the dry earth, slamming onto the taut nylon of the tent fly. Moments later the rain stops as quickly as it began, but the wind and the lightning continue. The thunder rumbles long and hard through the mountains and valleys. You know that the wind will make the fires harder to fight, and the lightning will probably set off some new blazes. All you can do now is wait it out, and check your tent to make sure the pegs are secure and the fly is set.

Lights out seemed early, even though it was the old standard 10:00 pm, or as they call it, 2200 hours. Nevertheless you can forget about sleep. You're still excited from your jump earlier in the day. The sensation of being suspended above the earth, of feeling like a species other than human, alive and free, is too much to allow you to sleep.

Suddenly you are aware of a scratching at the tent fly. It is a faint sound, but something is definitely there.

Turn to page 23.

You hear the sound of footsteps coming toward you. Although you want to escape, your body won't move. It is as if you've become a part of the earth, something silent and immobile.

The flashlight is shining right into your face. As you shield your eyes, you are pulled roughly to your feet, slapped several times, and pushed violently inside the parachute shed along with Bill.

Minutes later flames hungrily consume the dry old wood. The fire is so intense that the two of you don't stand a chance. However, it's the smoke that gets you before the flames do.

The End

48

Thirty minutes later you are standing on a rock, overlooking a shallow canyon. Scanning it carefully, you look for any signs of movement or color, any shape that would denote a human being. You find nothing.

Your digital wristwatch reads 4:52. Where did the time fly to? you ask yourself. A sense of panic begins to creep up on you. You try to push it aside, realizing now is not the time to lose control. Besides, everything is okay. You still have some time.

Then you see it, just a movement, nothing more. It's a small movement attached to something bright purple. It appears to be the nylon fabric of a hiking boot, and it protrudes a few inches beyond a jumble of rocks. You work your way over, and a few minutes later you reach the rocks.

"Holy moly!" you shout, surprised to find the body of a short man dressed in high-tech outdoor clothes. He's lying on his back, a dried rivulet of blood covering the side of his face and matting his hair. His eyes are closed, but he is breathing, although it's shallow and rapid. Once again he jerks his legs, his eyelids fluttering ever so lightly. Then they open.

Turn to page 110.

50

Pointing back down the trail, you see the flames coming from another fire. You are getting boxed in! "Let's head for the river!" you say,

Fear grips you for a moment, but then your survival instincts kick in, and you and Bill jump, run, stumble, and slide down the slope, heading toward the river. Small trees and brush block your way, but you manage to push past them. Twice you stumble over rocks and twigs, landing with a bone-rattling jolt on the slanted earth. Each time you pick yourself up, managing to push onward, running for your life.

Turn to page 112.

Fear rises up within you, and for a moment you dare not make a move. Time seems to stand still. Milt just stares you down, a thin smile on his lips. Suddenly you become aware of the beating of your heart and wonder if he can hear it, it seems so loud. Acting on instinct, you cautiously take one step back, then another, creating a space between you and your adversary.

"Hey! Where you going?" he asks. "You're not afraid of me now, are you? Why old Milt here wouldn't hurt a fly." He takes a step toward you, then he stops. Despite the playfulness of his words, he is not smiling.

"Milt, I've got to get on my way. They'll be expecting me soon. I promised I would check in with them before I headed back. If you don't want me to mention your friend, that's fine. But I've got to call and get going. How about it—the radio, please?" You surprise yourself by your sudden coolness and your ability to make this short speech.

"Okay, but I monitor the call. No secret messages. Got it?" Milt says, handing the radio over to you. Reason and instinct fight within you. Reason says to signal Haven, but your instinct says to play it straight.

If you decide to give Haven a signal, letting him know there's a problem, turn to page 92.

If you decide to play it straight, turn to page 74.

Turn to page 79.

Going against your better judgment, you decide to join Bill in tracking down these people in the parachute shed, whoever they may be. The joy of the day has evaporated, and there is danger in the air bordering on evil. You are afraid of what might happen.

"Follow me," Bill whispers; then he is off, circling the parachute shed.

You get as low to the ground as possible, then scurry after Bill. Coming up on the side of the shed, the two of you hunker down below one of the windows, which is unfortunately locked. The voices coming from inside are indistinct. You can't tell how many people are in there.

Suddenly the door opens, and two people step out. They look around in the darkness, then hurry off. Holding your breath, you freeze to the spot, all muscles tense. Bill is the same way. Gently you tap him on the arm and point to the open door.

"Shall we check inside? I think they're all gone."

"Okay. I'll go first," he replies, slipping along the wall, onto the porch, then in through the half-open doorway. You follow.

"Stop! Don't move," comes a thin voice. You stop in your tracks. A flashlight flicks on, cutting a hole in the darkness. It searches your face first, then Bill's.

"Kids. I might have known it. Well, you want to play with adults, then you'll play by the rules all right. Get going." He points toward the door.

Turn to page 75.

"I'll go, Porky. You stay here," you whisper. "I'll get Tomas, and we'll radio Brouillard for help."

"Listen, get the others—Nick, Dennis, and Marc. Tell them to surround the shed. Oh, and send someone to the plane. Hurry."

You slant off into the woods as quietly as possible, making a beeline for the cabins. This time you don't hesitate. You knock on the door of Tomas' cabin and enter without waiting.

He's not there. A quick check shows that his bed hasn't been slept in.

Maybe he has the night off, you speculate. You don't think much of it at first; however, it is a long way into town, you realize, and there isn't much there: two beer halls, a general store, one gas station, and a post office. Hardly worth calling it a town at all, but when you live out in the woods for a long stretch, anything begins to seem more and more like a city than a bump in the road, you reason.

You go on to Dennis' cabin, but he's not in either. The same with Marc. Maybe they're all out together, you think. Then an awful thought pops into your mind, one you'd rather not think of. What if these people are all in on this together?

Turn to page 43.

After eight or nine minutes you move slowly and cautiously from your hiding spot, then continue down the gully and head for the parking lot and the helicopter.

From overhead you hear the sound of the police bullhorn, *"Put your hands up! You cannot escape. This is the state police. Put down your weapon."*

A wave of relief comes over you. Stuff like this happens in the movies or on TV, but not to me, you think. You're about to get up to get a better look at the action when you stop where you are; no sense in getting mistaken for Milt, you realize.

"Walk this way nice and easy and nobody gets hurt."

The next thing you hear is your own name being called. They've got Milt; it's time to head in. Its been a long, hard day, but at least it's over, and you're safe.

The End

You decide to take the risk. Porky agrees, and goes for help.

"Hey, Bill, it's me. I'm all alone," you call out, your voice tinny.

"Okay, kid," says another voice, harsh and scratchy, which you don't recognize. "Come over here. Keep your hands away from your body where I can see them. There is a rifle trained on you."

You're lucky, they haven't realized that Porky has slipped away.

Fear invades every single molecule of your body, gripping your brain like a wrench, almost choking you. Gingerly you step forward. You feel as if the ground beneath your feet will crack like glass as you move forward, stepping into the unknown terror.

"Stay back!" Bill shouts at you. "These guys are killers."

You watch as Bill is felled by a vicious blow to the head with a gun butt. Instinctively, you dive for cover. Three bullets slice the air, thudding into the ground where you were standing just moments before. You scramble around the parachute shed, but before you can make it to the woods for safety, a stab of light catches you. You're caught!

"Don't you dare move another inch."

Turn to page 47.

58

Within two hours you reach the ridge on the topo map that Haven circled in red marker. The wind has picked up here, and you put on your windbreaker. "Time for lunch," you announce to yourself out loud.

"Mind if I join you?" comes a strange voice, startling you. A rugged man in his mid-thirties steps out from behind an outcropping of rock. He stands perfectly still, neither hostile nor particularly friendly. Here in the wilderness people, more than likely, are loners, thirsting for some company.

"Not at all." It's an awkward moment, but the stranger smiles and holds out his hand.

"Milt Lombard, from L.A. Glad to see you." He walks over to the large rock in front of you and sits down. "Say, I've got a little problem. Maybe you can help me."

"I'll try," you reply, suddenly sensing that something is wrong. Remaining alert, you manage to calm yourself, writing off the uneasiness to all of the excitement of the day.

"I'm supposed to meet a friend up in the canyon," Milt says. "I'm a day late, and unfortunately I've got to start heading back. Business, you know. I hate it, but it pays the bills." He smiles as he peels one of the oranges you've handed him. A wedge of cheddar cheese sits on a square of greasy paper—his contribution to lunch.

Turn to page 21.

The plane rolls down the dirt runway and slowly lifts off, climbing into the clear morning air. You are locked deep in thought, fighting fear and dealing with the mounting excitement inside you.

Twenty minutes later the plane has reached the proper altitude. It begins to circle in slow arcs, and you look out of the small rectangular window at the ground below. Everything looks so small when you are almost three thousand feet above it: trees, streams, cars, buildings. The mountains rise all around you to the north and west. If only you could just enjoy the view and not have to worry about jumping.

Suddenly a voice cuts through your reverie. It comes from a speaker mounted on the bulkhead separating the cargo hold from the pilot's cabin, and repeats, *"Approaching drop zone."*

A red light winks on and off above the cargo door through which you will soon step. Below the red light is a darkened green light. Yours are not the only eyes that are glued to these lights, waiting for your signal to jump.

Brouillard stands up. He does some last-minute adjusting to his equipment, tugging here and there on the harness and the webbing. Everyone else does the same. The first jump is to be a static line jump, he tells you. When you step out of the plane, all you have to worry about is the position of your body. The chute automatically opens when the rip cord, attached to the line in the plane, is pulled taut.

Turn to page 8.

"I need two of you to go for the police," you tell the group. "The phones are out. Tomas, Marc, Dennis, and the others aren't around. I don't know where they are, but right now I don't really care as long as they're out."

"What do you mean by that? a girl named Sally asks.

You are on the spot. "I can't find them. They must have the night off, or—who knows."

"No way!" Nick shouts. "You aren't going to tell me that you think they're in on this. If you are, then this must be a joke."

"Maybe that's the way they celebrate our first jump, you know, with some kind of crazy joke," someone else says.

"Maybe this is some kind of test," suggests another.

Several others in the group murmur with agreement.

"Then it doesn't matter. Two of you go for the police. Take one of the cars in the motor pool. The others come with me. Keep quiet, and spread out. We'll surround the cabin."

Go on to the next page.

Two people fade off toward the motor pool areas as you and the others move toward the parachute shed. The flashlight there has gone off, and all is quiet. Moments later you are back at the spot where you left Porky, only he is no longer there.

The darkness that surrounds you is overwhelming. Everything seems so quiet and calm, you half expect that if you went back to Bill's tent, he would be inside, safe and sleeping.

"So, what's up? I don't see nothin'," says a boy called Mickey.

"I don't know. But let's find out," you say, edging out from the cover of the woods and moving toward the parachute shed.

Turn to page 71.

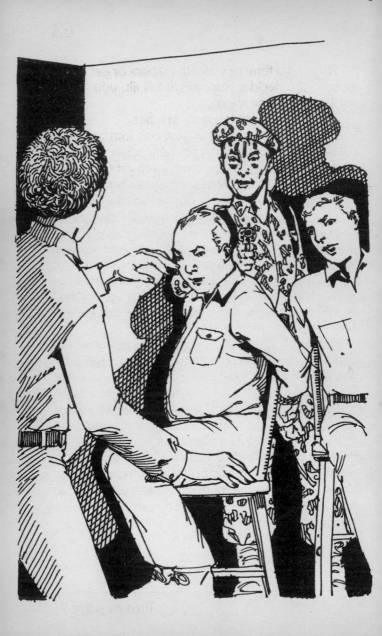

There's no time to wake the others or get to the police, you decide. Running at full tilt, you return to the parachute shed.

"Porky. Hey, Pork," you whisper.

"He's in here, kid. I suggest you join us."

As if in a dream, you cross the open area and mount the steps of the porch. Common sense tells you to run away as fast as you can go, but you stay where you are. Jumping out of the plane was a cinch compared to this.

The door opens slowly, revealing a short, paunchy man with a snub-nosed revolver pointed at you. "Be my guest, please," he says, motioning you inside. This whole scene smacks of some low-grade television drama—guns, hostages—it all seems so crazy. Nothing makes sense. Your world has suddenly gone topsy-turvy.

You reach down inside yourself for strength and calmness in order to continue. It's a pretty far reach, and all that you come up with is a lot more fear.

Inside, you find Porky and Bill sitting in chairs, their hands bound behind them. The man with the gun is next to them, a smile on his face. He looks to be in his midforties and is dressed in a camouflage outfit, the type you buy in the army-navy surplus stores. He has streaks of black greasepaint over his face and is wearing gloves and a small pack.

Turn to page 9.

You manage to set aside your fears as best you can and decide to go through with the jump after all.

"Ten seconds to drop," the pilot announces. The red light then blinks off and the green light comes on.

"Everybody hooked up?" Porky asks. Everybody nods, checking to see that they are hooked up to the static line. You see Bill, and he gives you the thumbs-up signal. He looks calm, and you envy him, although he's probably feeling the same as, if not worse than, you are.

"Let's go!" Brouillard shouts. The first person steps out without hesitation, then the second, and then the third. But the fourth person hesitates, his fingers gripping the side of the fuselage. Brouillard unhooks him from the static line, and he steps aside as the rest of you continue with the jump.

Turn to page 70.

Speed is important. You run across the open land, taking a shortcut through a stand of pine, until you finally reach the motor pool area. There are three vehicles in the lot. Two are 4x4 pickup trucks, and the third is a huge U.S. Army six-wheeler, now used to haul supplies, equipment, and firefighters.

"Keys! Where do they keep the keys?" you yell out loud with frustration. Slow down. Use your brains. Where would you hide a key if you had to? you ask yourself. I'd just stick it under the front seat. Yeah, that's what I'd do. No one expects anyone to steal anything out here.

Reaching under the front seat of the first 4x4, you come up with nothing other than some candy wrappers and a few straws from a fast-food shake.

Rats! You move to the next 4x4. Again nothing.

"I don't want to drive that monster," you say, surveying the six-wheeler. "Oh, well, here goes nothing." Your dad taught you how to drive a jeep when your feet could barely touch the pedals. You practiced in the fields behind the farm. It's been a long time since then, but you're sure you can still do it. What choice do you have, really?

The climb up into the cab itself is a task. But there, right in the ignition, is a key hanging, waiting for you. After turning the key to light the cab, you examine the dashboard. Sure enough, there is a manual choke. You pull it out about halfway, pump the accelerator, hold it to the floor, and then turn the key all the way.

Turn to page 11.

The sound of several helicopters interrupts Tomas. You watch as two state police choppers land outside the shed and Brouillard steps off.

"We radioed them from the plane," Tomas says, grinning ear to ear.

Brouillard and the police take over. With dawn not too far away, everyone finally returns to their tents.

"There'll be no jump this morning," Brouillard announces. "But be ready tomorrow."

Right now jumping is the farthest thing from your mind. All you can do as you climb into bed is think about sleep and the peace that it brings.

The End

You find that it is difficult to concentrate fully on what Porky and the instructor are saying. You know that you should pay attention, but the excitement of the day obscures their words. Your mind drifts back to the incredible feeling of being in the air, being a part of it, moving slowly toward earth and being able to control your path as if you were flying.

The instructor is talking about the dangers of dropping into a fire zone. He mentions the rising air currents, called thermals, and explains how difficult they are to judge.

In the midst of this talk, Brouillard strides into the room. "I need two volunteers," he announces in a measured but excited tone. All attention is focused on him instantly; even Porky and the instructor are waiting on his next words.

"We've got a problem," Brouillard says. "About sixty miles northwest of here there are a couple of small fires, nothing big. Local groups should have them under control soon, but you can't bet on that. We've got to check the situation out. As you know, our other regulars are on that big burn up on Bear Creek. I need two volunteers to come with me. Any takers?"

Turn to page 84.

Coming upon the clearing, your feet touch the ground, and you land, just the way you were taught to do in jump class. Crablike you scuttle out from under the blades. As the copter sets down, the rotors come to a whining stop.

"You okay?" Brouillard shouts, jumping out of the craft and running toward you. Concern and care are all over his face, and you are reminded of your father.

"Yeah, I'm all right, for the most part. But how did you know I was in trouble?"

Brouillard offers you a canteen, and you both take a sip. "Instinct. Some campers reported a strange guy in your area. I just started to worry. Sometimes you have to trust what you feel, so I decided to check out the area. That's when we found you."

"But that crazy back there, he got away," you say.

"Don't worry, the troopers have got him by now. Come, we have a fire to put out."

The End

70

It's your turn, and suddenly you find yourself falling! Your chute opens with a snap and fills with air, straining against your shoulders. You hang in the air, gently falling toward the beautiful world below. The parafoil supports you; from bunched-up, multicolored nylon, it has swelled into a ribbed, rectangular shape that functions similarly to the wing of a plane. It is very different from the old round parachutes. These can be directed with much greater precision, and the landing, if done right, can be gentle enough for you to hit the earth without much shock to your feet.

Your spirits are rising; you've done it! Looking all around, you see the red and yellow parafoils of the others. A feeling of exhilaration and well-being overcomes you, but you remember what Porky and Brouillard have drummed into your head. "Be awake! Concentrate! You're not sightseeing!" Maintaining your excitement, you focus your attention on the wind and the rapidly approaching ground.

Turn to page 5.

Suddenly there is a coughing, sputtering sound. Then it catches and turns into a hammering, throaty roar as it rips through the darkness.

"It's the plane! They're in the plane!" someone yells.

The number two engine turns over, stammers a bit, and then falls into its rhythm. The landing lights come on, and you can both see and hear the big plane taxiing down the strip, positioning itself into the wind for takeoff.

Then a voice comes from a radio inside the parachute shed. *"We have a full load of hostages. I repeat. We have a full load of hostages."*

You dash into the shed. There you find the radio phone sitting on a packing table, sqawking out the message.

"What are your demands?" you ask, keying the transmit button.

There is a moment of scratchy noise and then the voice comes back, "Very simple. We want you to fire the camp."

"You must be joking," you say back incredulously at the enormity and the stupidity of the demand.

"Maybe you would rather talk to the one called Porky?"

Porky's voice comes over the radio. It is thin and reflects great tension and fear.

Turn to page 34.

A muffled groan comes from the bedroom.

"Porky!" you shout, running across the room in three steps. The door is blocked. "It's me, Porky. It's me!" you shout, pushing against the door gently. Slowly it opens. Porky's body, you discover, is blocking the door. He is all trussed up, like a calf ready for branding, a red polka-dot bandana tied securely around his mouth. His eyes are open, filled with both anger and fear. Within moments you have him free.

"Did you see them?" he gulps after you remove the gag.

"Yes, they're in the parachute shed."

"Good lord! Let's go."

"What happened?"

"Later—we've got to stop them." Porky is off and running. Despite his bulky size, he covers ground fast, and you have trouble keeping up. Moments later you are at the parachute shed. It is silent.

You reach out and stop Porky. "Bill's some-where around here. He was keeping an eye on them while I went and got you. Let's find him first."

Unfortunately, you don't have an opportunity to go and look for him. A flashlight rips through the darkness, shining on Bill, who is standing in the doorway of the parachute shed.

Turn to page 25.

Deciding to play it straight, you attempt to contact Haven. There's a lot of static on the air, and although it's frustrating, you keep trying. Milt keeps a close eye on you, and you wish you were anywhere else but here. Eventually you get through and make contact.

"Haven, it's me. Everything is A-OK. I'll be heading out close to our original estimated time of arrival, 10–4."

Turning to Milt, you give him a questioning look. "Okay? See, no problems," you say. "What's with you anyway?"

That was a big mistake. Milt's face turns bright red. "What's with *you*, kid? Listen, you mind your own business, you hear? You'll stay healthy that way." He has lost all of the polish he had during his first encounter with you. Given his mood swings, it's as though he has two personalities.

"Hey, I didn't mean anything by that. I'm sorry, guess I'm just tired. It's been a long day."

"Well, it's going to be longer. Let's move out. Remember, no funny stuff, right?"

"Anything you say, Milt. But—where are we going?"

"You really don't learn, do you, kid? Button that lip." Milt heads along the ridge at high speed. You do your best to follow, stumbling several times along the way.

Turn to page 105.

Your instinct tells you to make a dash for the woods, and you could probably get away, but unfortunately you are not alone. Bill would suffer the consequences if you managed to get away and he didn't.

The moment and the opportunity pass quickly as you leave the wooded path and emerge on the landing strip next to the old DC–3. It looms in the darkness like some ancient dinosaur, its head pointed up, arms outstretched, and its tail down on the earth.

"In you go," comes a command. Once inside, your hands are bound with nylon parachute cord. The two of you are then hooked to the static line, only this time without a parachute. The big radial engines tick over, then burst into life. Slowly the plane starts down the runway.

You wish this were a nightmare, but you know it isn't. You can't believe what is happening.

"Who are you? What do you want?" you manage to ask.

Turn to page 86.

"Okay, I suppose I can look for your friend. I have to go up to that canyon anyway. Tell me more," you say.

Reaching into his pack, Milt withdraws a compass, binoculars and a topo map similar to the one Haven gave you. He is all business now, and you watch him carefully, noting every facial expression and hand movement. Observation is very important. Sometimes the smallest detail can yield a great deal of information. You notice an intensity in this man that fascinates you. He is far from being relaxed. He is like a man on a mission.

"My friend's name is Tim. Tim Martinez. Doesn't know his way around the woods. We left five days ago. He's probably frantic by now."

"What's he doing in the woods then?" you ask.

"Trying to prove something, I guess. He read some article on survival, gets this idea in his head. The next thing I know we're heading off for these here woods. He decides to go solo for five days, saying we'll meet at this spot which he picks out on the map."

"Has he got supplies and a sleeping bag?"

"Yes to the bag, but he's probably running low on supplies by now."

"Here, let's look at your map," you say.

Turn to page 19.

It's bound to take you almost an hour to cover the five miles. You hoof it as fast as you can, but by the time you finally make it to the camp, everything is over and the police are wrapping things up. Bill fills you in on what happened.

"They call themselves environmental terrorists," he says. "They threaten to destroy forests unless they're paid a ransom. These guys are nuts."

"Yeah, but they almost got away with it," you reply.

The image of blazing forests and frightened hostages fills your mind. This has been enough for you for one day. It's time to get some sleep.

The End

"Yeah, well, real estate sounds fine and all that, but I'm an environmentalist, myself," you tell Milt, trying to assert yourself a little.

"Oh, I see. Monkey Wrench Gang kind of person, eh? You don't care for developers, is that it? I guess you'd rather save some tree than create jobs and make money."

You don't like the run of this conversation. His tone is enough to tell you that this man is no environmentalist, and that he doesn't take you very seriously. And yet, you know you shouldn't judge too quickly. First impressions are more often pretty accurate, but you've been wrong lots of times too. Take Bill, for example. When you first met him, you thought he was a snotty, upper-class Eastern preppy. You wouldn't even give him the time of day. Now he's your best friend here in Idaho, someone you'll probably know for a long time. You decide to respect your instincts about Milt, be wary, but give him a chance.

"Some developers are all right," you say. "We need more housing and jobs. I've no objection to those things if they're done right."

"Well, who gets to decide what's right, you?" Milt looks at you questioningly, but with a glint in his eye. He's toying with you, you can tell, and you want to end the conversation before it gets out of hand. Not only that, it's getting late, and you don't want to be up in the mountains after sunset. It's not that you're afraid; you're not. It's just that you still have to finish your patrol and then hook up with Haven and Bill.

Turn to page 16.

Before the message is completed Brouillard is already at the helicopter. Moments later he is airborne and away.

You stare at the quickly receding copter, wondering what is next. But you don't have to wonder for long. The ranger finishes up with his message on the radio and turns toward you and Bill.

"Name's Haven," he says to you, introducing himself. "I've got to send a patrol out along that rim over there," he continues, pointing to the distant horizon and getting down to business. "We've had a report that there might be some campers over there. If this fire spreads it could be bad. I also need help with the fire we've got going right here. It's almost under control, but our men need a break. We could use some new blood."

You've gone from first jump to firefighting and patrols all in the same day. Your dad always prepared you to accept change and to be flexible in developing situations, but you think you might be stepping in over your head here. You're not scared; its just that things are moving fast, almost too fast. What will you do?

If you decide to go on patrol, turn to page 28.

If you decide to help the rangers with the fire, turn to page 38.

Sick with fear, you and the others fan out and put match to paper, pine needles, and brush. The flames are greedy. You watch as the entire camp burns to the ground. Overhead, the engines of the DC–3 grow fainter and fainter as the plane heads north in the direction of Canada.

Weeks later the wreckage of the DC–3 is found high in the Canadian Rockies. There are no survivors.

The End

"What are pilgrims?" you ask Haven.

Haven laughs. "Oh, just a nickname we have for tourists. Nothing bad really, it's just that they're so earnest, seeing this country for the first time. Anyway, let's head out. Time's a-wastin'."

The last sentence about time catches you by surprise. It's one of your father's expressions, and it stops you in your tracks to hear it come from someone else.

You pile into the beat-up Chevy Blazer with Bill and Haven. The ride to the burn area is bumpy, and Haven drives fast. Holding on to the stanchions of the roll bar is all you can do to keep from falling out. This almost-youthful aggressiveness behind the wheel is a dimension of Haven's personality you didn't expect. He otherwise seems so deliberate and measured.

Turn to page 102.

84

Everyone's hand shoots up. Brouillard surveys the group, pleased with the response. "There is a downside to this mission," he continues. "Whoever goes will miss two or three days of jump training. We'll do our best, but you'll be missing time, and all of you know the rules. To qualify, you have to complete all the jumps. Unfortunately this will delay your certification as a smoke jumper until we can reschedule the jumps you missed. Any takers still?"

The opportunity is certainly an exciting one, but you're not sure if you want to delay your certification. After all, that's what you've been working for. The more you think about it, however, the more you realize that the bottom line in your decision to train is to put out fires and save lives. And this is your chance. Rescheduling the jumps wouldn't be the worst thing that could happen to you. The experience you would gain from going on this fire could only be valuable and would certainly look good on your record.

Whatever your decision, you'll have to make it now.

If you decide to volunteer and go with Brouillard, turn to page 12.

If you decide to stay with the jump class, turn to page 17.

Frightening images begin to race through your mind, and terror prevents you from taking action. You stare at Milt, your eyes more focused and intent than they've ever been before. You seem to be able to see right through him, right into the heart and soul of this man. What you find there is a deep sorrow and loneliness. You can see that he is a man haunted by his own fantasies and his own failures. As you search his face, you do not sense that he is evil or truly violent. The way to handle Milt, you realize, is through kindness and understanding.

You begin to speak. "Well, Milt, you must be feeling really bad about something. You know, we all feel bad at times. My dad always said that problems always seem smaller once you talk them out."

Milt eyes you suspiciously for a moment, then slowly begins to tell you the long story of his life. You keep him talking, hoping that Haven will come looking for you, but you're not sure for how much longer you can keep this up.

The End

The man with the thin voice hesitates, then replies, "Let's just say we are some businessmen making an investment. The two of you will be our guarantees. I'm sure someone cares for you. Let's just see how much."

The plane lurches into the air and begins a slow circle above the camp with a radius of about two miles. Intermittently the clouds break apart, and moonlight dents the dark interior.

An hour later, with gas running low, the men grow angry and more and more frustrated. Having received no response to their demands, they hurl you and Bill out into the emptiness of the sky. Unlike this afternoon, your landing won't be smooth. Fortunately, you don't have to worry about what will happen to you for much longer.

The End

"Oh, almost forgot. You got a flashlight?" Haven asks. As anxious as he is to be on his way, you can sense that he is a careful man.

"Sure thing. It's small, but good," you reply, patting your side. It's the one you got from your dad for your thirteenth birthday.

"Good luck. Stay calm. Radio me if you need to. Remember, don't take any risks. And if you see any sign of fire, beat it. Get yourself right back here, okay?"

"You can be sure of it." you reply.

Haven flashes you a half-grin then heads off for the fire. You hold yourself back for several minutes, trying to clear your mind of all the events that have been jumbling together in the recent hours. Taking a deep breath, you try to reach down within yourself and come up with a sense of calm and well-being. You imagine a still forest pond; it's a trick your dad taught you. You think of the pond—its calmness, its depth, and its beauty. Focusing, you see almost no ripples. You hear no sound. Your heart steadies its beat and slows down. Your mind clears, and your thoughts are focused. Now you are ready.

Turn to page 33.

"So, big deal," you say. "A couple of strangers. Why, they're probably just friends of Brouillard's."

"No, they weren't friends of anyone here. They were messing around with our equipment," Bill says.

"What do you mean? Were they stealing?"

"Worse—sabotage. At least that's what I think they were doing. I first saw them out by the plane. They were messing around inside. I couldn't tell exactly what was going on. There were no lights, but I heard a lot of whispering."

"Then what?"

"They—" Bill suddenly peers around the tent and squints into the dark. "Hey, I think they're in the parachute shed."

"Let's get Porky!" you say.

"No, let's find out what they're up to first and track them back to their vehicle."

It's a hard decision. Caution dictates going to Porky for help, action says to follow these people before they get away.

"Are you coming with me?" Bill asks.

If you decide to go for Porky, turn to page 24.

If you decide to stay with Bill and investigate, turn to page 53.

The scenery below speeds past you. Thirty-five minutes later, you circle a patch of smoke. Brouillard points to it, nods his head, and searches for a landing area. He spots one, a break in the trees cut just for this purpose, over by two men signaling with a yellow groundsheet. Swiftly the Alouette heads down.

When the rotors come to rest, the three of you climb out, greeted by the smell of freshly cut pine and woodsmoke. The two smells bring back memories of camping trips with your dad when you were younger. He always took you and your sister up into northern Canada to canoe and fish for two weeks every summer, from age seven until you were fourteen. That last summer was the best. You caught a salmon that was record size—at least in your family—and the memory and pain of your parents' divorce seemed to have faded. It felt really good being out in the woods and lakes, and you had a lot of fun. That's what families are all about, you've always thought: enjoying each others' company, sticking together, and no fighting. That was one of your dad's rules. Arguments were okay, he would always say, but fighting was out; he wouldn't tolerate it. Not quite two months after that trip your dad was killed.

You are flooded with emotion, and tears begin to well up. You try to blot out the memory of those days and get hold of yourself, focusing on the mission that lies ahead of you.

Turn to page 13.

Keying the radio for transmit, you go ahead with your call to Haven, deciding to add a twist. You're going to need help and can't afford to rely on Milt's pretenses of being harmless.

"Canyon Patrol Two calling Tomas. Repeat, Canyon Patrol Two calling Tomas. Can you read me? Over," you say, acting as natural as possible. There is static on the radio; you try again. "Tomas, this is Canyon Patrol Two, come in, Tomas. Ears are open." You hope that Haven will pick up on your call for Tomas. Tomas never leaves base camp; Haven should read it as a signal that things are not normal.

Once again there's static on the line, then it clears and you hear Haven's voice. It is an instant comfort to you. Milt moves closer to you, keeping a careful eye on you.

"Canyon Two, we read you loud and clear. Tomas not available. Do you have a message for him?"

"Mission unsuccessful. Cancel pickup. Tell Tomas that there's nobody out here and I'm on my way back. Over and out," you say.

"Over."

You turn to Milt. "Okay?"

Go on to the next page.

He nods, "Listen, kid, I don't want to scare you, but I think you'd better come with me. It's no big deal, but I don't think you should be roaming around these parts, what with the fire and all. I'd feel kinda responsible if anything happened to you."

You stare at Milt, stunned by how delusional he is. "You wish to protect me?" you say. "You've got it all backward, I'm afraid. I'm here to look after your welfare. I'm with the ranger service, got it?" Your brief contact with Haven has given you some renewed courage. If he picked up your message, he'll be on your trail soon enough.

Turn to page 96.

You wait a few minutes to be sure Milt is out of hearing range. Then, unslinging your backpack from your shoulder, you remove the radio and switch it to "transmit." Using the proper wavelength, you call, "Ridge patrol to Haven. Can you read me?" You wait for a response, but there is only the usual static on the radio.

Keying the transmit button, you begin again. "Ridge patrol to—"

"Well, little buddy, I figured you'd try somethin' smart like that," Milt says, coming up from behind you. "I don't like that. No, I don't. I don't like that one little bit, and I'm going to have to do something about it."

Petrified, you watch Milt remove a Colt magnum from his pack. Despite his earlier words, he sure seems to know how to handle a gun, you think.

"Hand over the radio," he demands.

Turn to page 85.

"Sure thing," Milt says. "I'm sorry. I forgot myself for a moment. You lead the way, but I'll tell you where we're going. So, less talk, let's get moving." Milt points off in the direction of the road ahead.

You heave a sigh of relief. This is exactly where you wanted to head. It is the logical place Haven will come to look for you first. You stride off, feeling more and more confident with each step that brings you closer to the rough-cut parking lot. Thinking back, you seem to remember a beat-up 4x4 parked at the far end of the road. Maybe that's Milt's vehicle.

You find the walking easy, but you try to slow the pace down to allow Haven the time he needs to get to you. Milt keeps quiet, and you wonder just how crazy he really is. You decide that it's best not to try and find out. Let sleeping dogs lie was one of your father's favorite proverbs, and you decide to follow it. Suddenly you wish he were here with you right now. You feel an overwhelming wave of sadness and fear, and an involuntary shudder passes over you.

"Hey, kid! You cold or something? You're shivering. Want a sweater?"

Go on to the next page.

Boy, this guy doesn't miss a thing, you say to yourself. "No, just tired. It's been a long day. Started out with a jump this morning." You're not sure why you told him that. It would probably be best not to talk with this guy too much.

"Jump? Don't tell me they're letting kids like you jump these days."

"Hey, I'm not a kid. I'm old enough. I qualify."

"Sorry. Didn't mean to offend you. I'm qualified to jump myself. Green Beret. The Nam. Two tours." He pauses for a moment.

Turn to page 26.

You decide to listen to your inner voice and give in to your fears. With the courage of your own convictions, you unhook yourself from the static line and move over to Brouillard.

"I can't jump," you say, feeling shame and fear mingle in the flush on your face.

"That's okay. It happens to lots of people. Nothing to be ashamed of. Sit here," he says, moving over a little so you can sit next to him.

No one says anything, the roar of the engine filling the void. You're feeling embarrassed, but everything is going to be all right, you tell yourself.

"Okay, jumpers, get ready," Porky says, standing up and moving over to the open cargo door. The green light is on, and one by one the others move to the opening, as if in a trance, and jump. You watch as they fall, their parachutes opening swiftly and colorfully.

Obeying some command coming from deep within you, you stand, reaching up and hooking yourself back onto the static line.

The next thing you know you are at the cargo door. Without another moment of hesitation, you jump, feeling yourself free-falling. Your chute opens, and you gracefully approach the earth, enjoying the thrill of the jump and the beauty of the view that surrounds you.

The End

"This is my best yet!" he shouts, scrambling back up the slope to where you are standing in horror. "Just look at those flames."

In the distance you hear the clack of rotor blades. You look at Milt, but he is so engrossed in the fire, his eyes aglow, that you decide it's time for you to depart.

Running for your life, you skim the ridge, dive into the woods, skirt a stream and a gully, and reach the parking area at the end of the logging road. It doesn't look like Milt has run after you, but as a precaution, you take cover behind a pile of logs.

Moments later the copter lands, Brouillard at the controls and Haven in the right-hand seat. You dash for it, and at just that moment, Milt makes a break for it, running through the trees. There is a gun in his hand, and its barrel is aimed at you!

"Hang on!" Brouillard shouts, and with full power the helicopter climbs into the sky. Hanging on to the skids of the helicopter with all your might, you are whipped into the air, dangling high above the treetops. Milt recedes from view, an angry spot doing a dance of rage, pointing his weapon helplessly at the sky. For a moment you close your eyes, afraid to look; then the exhilaration of the moment and the joy of the escape overcome your timidity. You open your eyes, looking down at the trees below you. The helicopter speeds off, and soon you are over a clearing, away from Milt and all his madness.

Turn to page 68.

"Let's see what Haven says," you say to Bill. "You stay here. Keep that guy in sight. I'll go up the trail and get Haven, okay?"

"Sure, boss," Bill says, throwing you a smart salute.

"Hey, I'm just making a suggestion."

"Well your *suggestion,* as you call it, sounds suspiciously like a command to me. Nature abhors a vacuum, and you just love to fill those vacuums."

"Hey, ease up. I'm sorry. I didn't mean to be bossy."

"Well you are, sometimes," Bill says, lowering his voice a notch. You can tell that the fight is over. You feel bad that you hurt his feelings. Still, you are just about to counter with the criticism that he occasionally acts and talks like a preppy snob. But reason takes over, and you say nothing. One thing has nothing to do with the other.

"So, why don't we flip for it?" you suggest, taking a coin from your pocket.

"Great. I'll take heads."

You flip the coin, watching as it spins in the air, the sun catching it for just a split second and reflecting off the silver. It hits the ground with a thunk.

"Heads. You got it," you say.

"Great, you go after Haven, and I'll stay," he says.

"Hey, wait a minute, I thought—"

"Well, don't. I was going to stay anyway. I just don't like being bossed around and told what to do. Go."

Turn to page 39.

Forty minutes later you roll into a makeshift staging area where several other vehicles are parked. The smell of smoke is particularly heavy here, and the wind has picked up, sweeping down the narrow valley toward the fire.

"Okay," Haven says, "you got safety gear, helmets, goggles, fire-retardant jacket. Let me see your boots." Haven checks them, making sure they are the kind with special insulation used for jumping and fires, which they are. "Here, you'll need these," he says, tossing shovels at you and Bill. The three of you also take your packs, canteens, and a limited amount of food. One radio is handed out, and Bill takes it. "Remember, the two of you, don't get split up. Stay in contact with the main group at all times. Fire can be really tricky. Just be careful."

As you hit the trail you realize it's not really a trail, but a contour that snakes around rock outcroppings, drops down to the river, crosses it, and heads up the other side. It is steep, and your footing is unsure. Haven pushes ahead, and you and Bill do your best to try and keep up.

Turn to page 40.

"Oh, so we're on our own. Thanks a lot, Haven," you say, but there's nothing but smoke. Then you head back to Bill. When you reach him, he's sitting down, a handkerchief soaked in water covering his nostrils. You follow suit, soaking your bandana to get some relief from the acrid smoke.

The smoke begins to fill the narrow river valley. You can see across to the ridge, but there is no longer any sign of the figure.

"Where'd he go?"

"Beats me," Bill replies. "Now what?"

"Haven said to check it out, but what do we check out? That guy can see the fire as well as we can; and it's spreading. I say we call Haven and report a negative on the sighting."

You key the transmit button and call Haven. It takes a while to reach him, and when you do, you don't have a chance to explain. "Get out!" he commands. "Repeat! Get out, now! This thing is out of control."

By now you are starting to feel the heat, and you can see flames along with the smoke.

"What about the others? Is there anyone left out here?" Bill asks.

"I don't know, Bill," you say, "but I'll tell you one thing: we're in trouble. Look."

Turn to page 50.

Forty minutes later, the two of you stand above a valley of virgin pine. It's a beautiful sight, and for a brief moment you forget that you are a prisoner.

"Wow! This is beautiful," you say. "Those trees, they're unbelievable looking."

Milt smiles at you. He stands with his feet wide apart and his hands on his hips, his eyes shining. "It will be even more beautiful when I get through with it."

You watch as he removes from his pack an aluminum canister that is used to hold fuel for mountain stoves. He also holds a pack of all-weather matches, the kind that are coated with wax so they won't get wet.

"Okay, pal, now watch this."

Horror overwhelms you as you realize that he is going to start a fire and torch the forest. You begin to speak, but you can't. This is a nightmare, and you are helpless to do anything to stop him.

Milt slides down the steep sidewall until he reaches the trees. He gathers pine needles, old branches, and odd pieces of brush. Within a few minutes he has a sizeable pile of dry, flammable material.

"Ready, aim, fire!" Milt shouts, after pouring gasoline from the canister. You watch helplessly as the match flares, then drops onto the gasoline-soaked brush. There is a whumping sound as the gas ignites and the flame explodes. Milt looks up in triumph.

Turn to page 100.

106

You hesitate for a few moments, deciding not to make the call. You don't want to be an alarmist. I'll go it on my own, you say to yourself. There's no problem.

You get down to business. The spot where Milt's friend might be is indicated on the map. You'll have to go over the ridge, down a scree slope, and across a stream before you end up in the canyon area. If you move fast, you'll be able to make it in an hour or so, leaving just enough time for you to retreat by sunset. If you stop right now, you know that fatigue will set in and get the better of you.

The sun overhead is warm, your stomach is moderately full, and once again there is an air of excitement about your work. It is possible that the fire could spread, and this man, Tim Martinez, could be trapped. And so could you for that matter. Time is truly of the essence, and you urge yourself on.

The feeling that someone is following you eventually leaves you, and you feel relieved, with a renewed sense of confidence. It's a little tricky as you go along, making your way among the scree, loose rock, thick brush, and wind. You notice that the wind has picked up a little. You wonder exactly how far away that fire was that Bill and the other rangers went off to fight. On the topo it didn't look too far, maybe two ridges over. A little too close for comfort. Hopefully the wind won't feed the fire further to your direction.

Turn to page 48.

"Lets investigate this guy. It's not far, and he looks like he needs help. The fire's not coming from over there. We'll be safe," you say to Bill, aware that he is hesitant. You, however, are anxious to get going. Time could be very important.

Bill shakes his head. "I don't know. Haven said not to get separated."

"Yeah, but he meant you and me. Besides, he went ahead and left us. Hey, it is not like we're in the fire zone. Come, lets go."

"I'm staying; you go," Bill says.

You remember how stubborn he can get, almost defiant. "Fine," you decide. "I won't be long. Tell Haven where I am. I'll catch up with you later."

For a moment you hesitate, wondering whether or not you are doing the right thing or whether you're being foolish. "What the heck," you say.

It doesn't take you long to get to the other side of the river, although the water is a little rough. Even though it's low because of the almost-drought conditions, the current is fast and the rocks are slippery. You make it, and soon you are scrambling up the other side.

Within forty minutes you reach the spot where you saw the figure, only to find nobody there.

"Hey! Yo! Hey, where are you?" you shout, only to get a faint echo in return. You are alone, you realize, and whoever it was is now gone. For the next twenty minutes, you search the area without success, feeling increasingly angry and a little foolish.

Turn to page 42.

Now it's your turn! The ground is coming up awfully fast. Instinctively you adjust the risers the way you have practiced; with a moderate jolt you are on the ground and standing. The others follow; almost evenly they are divided between those who take a tumble and those who don't. No one is hurt.

You watch as Porky and Brouillard land. You are feeling so excited with your accomplishment that you want to climb right back into the jump plane and do it again.

"Well done, all of you!" Brouillard says as he goes from person to person, shaking hands and slapping backs. "Congratulations, you're all jumpers now."

The rest of the day is spent in small groups, discussing the jump and watching videotapes for review. You have other jumps scheduled in the next days, two from the same altitude, and more from a lower altitude, stressing the control of the chute and picking your landing spot.

Turn to page 67.

"Who are you? Where am I?" the man asks.

"It's okay. You'll be fine. Just take it easy," you say, kneeling down next to him. You check his pulse and examine his pupils for signs of a concussion.

"Can you count backward from ten?" you ask, a useful test to see if there is any injury to the brain.

The man responds, counting off slowly but easily.

"What happened to you?" you ask, anticipating his answer and fearing the worst.

"There was this crazy man. He was really weird. Met him two days ago."

Automatically you look around the area, scanning for any signs of Milt. Unfortunately—or fortunately—you see nothing.

"Was he from L.A.? Was his name Milt?" you ask.

"Yeah, that's the guy. He was a real nut case. He raved about all kinds of crazy stuff, politics, the homeless, the rich, environmentalists. I couldn't tell where he was coming from."

"And you never saw him before you met him here?" you ask.

Go on to the next page.

"Never saw him before and never want to see him again. By the way my name's—"

"—Tim Martinez," you say, finishing his sentence.

"Hey, how did you know that? Wait a minute, you're not a friend of that guy's, are you?" Suddenly there is a mixture of fear and wariness on his face.

"No, don't worry. I ran into him up on the ridge about two hours ago. It was really weird. He told me about you. Said you were buddies from L.A. Sent me here to try and find you."

Turn to page 30.

112

With a plunge, you and Bill finally reach the river. The water is shallow, but you're not hurt, and you manage to swim along until you find a fairly deep pool.

"What do you think?" Bill asks.

The smoke settles above you, and hot air rushes down the river. You need to duck under the water every so often to keep yourselves cool.

"We'll make it, don't worry. Let's just stay calm. This thing should be beyond us soon enough."

Just then you hear Haven. You turn to see him and six or seven of his men sloshing down the riverbed.

High above you, standing on the ridge, you think you see the figure of the man you spotted earlier. He seems to be jumping up and down, dancing, and you think you hear him laughing. You know that this man has something to do with the fire; if only you could reach him and find out for sure. The fire, meanwhile, roars on, making its way down the valley. For now you are safe.

The End

ABOUT THE AUTHOR

R.A. MONTGOMERY is a graduate of Williams College. He also studied in graduate programs at Yale University and New York University. After serving in a variety of administrative capacities at Williston Academy and Columbia University, he cofounded the Waitsfield Summer School in 1965. Following that, Mr. Montgomery helped found a research and development firm specializing in the development of educational programs. He worked for several years as a consultant to the Peace Corps in Washington, D.C., and West Africa. He is now both a writer and a publisher.

ABOUT THE ILLUSTRATOR

LESLIE MORRILL is a designer and illustrator whose work has won him numerous awards. He has illustrated over thirty books for children, including the Bantam Classic edition of *The Wind in the Willows*. Mr. Morrill has illustrated many books in the Skylark Choose Your Own Adventure series, including *Home in Time for Christmas, You See the Future, Stranded!,* and *You Can Make A Difference*. He has also illustrated *The First Olympics, The Perfect Planet, Hurricane!, Inca Gold, Stock Car Champion, Alien, Go Home!, Grave Robbers, The Treasure of the* Onyx Dragon, and *Fight For Freedom* in the Choose Your Own Adventure series. Mr. Morrill also illustrated both Super Adventure books, *Journey to the Year 3000* and *Danger Zones*.

Choosy Kids Choose

CHOOSE YOUR OWN ADVENTURE ®

Bantam Books, Dept. AV8, 414 East Golf Road, Des Plaines, IL 60016

Please send me the items I have checked above. I am enclosing $_____
(please add $2.00 to cover postage and handling). Send check or money
order, no cash or C.O.D.s please.

Mr/Ms _____

Address _____

City/State _____ Zip _____

AV8-2/90

Please allow four to six weeks for delivery.
Prices and availability subject to change without notice.

CHOOSE YOUR OWN ADVENTURE®